Ashley Small & ASHLEE TALL

BRUSHES
and
BASKETBALLS

by Michele Jakubowski

Illustrated by Hédi Fekete

PICTURE WINDOW BOOKS
a capstone imprint

Ashley Small and Ashlee Tall is published by Picture Window Books.
A Capstone Imprint
1710 Roe Crest Drive
North Mankato, Minnesota 56003
www.mycapstone.com

Library of Congress Cataloging-in-Publication Data
Names: Jakubowski, Michele, author. | Fekete, Hédi, illustrator.
Title: Brushes and basketballs / by Michele Jakubowski ; [illustrator, Hédi Fekete].
Description: North Mankato, Minnesota : Capstone Press, 2016. | © 2017 |
Series: Ashley Small and Ashlee Tall | Summary: Ever since the Taylors
moved out of the apartment building Ashley Sanchez and Ashlee Taylor
have been looking for something they could do together—they try basketball
and painting class, but somehow their skills do not quite match.
Identifiers: LCCN 2015049076| ISBN 9781515800101 (library binding) | ISBN
9781515800149 (pbk.) | ISBN 9781515800187 (ebook (pdf))
Subjects: LCSH: Moving, Household—Juvenile fiction. | Best
friends—Juvenile fiction. | Difference (Psychology)—Juvenile fiction. | CYAC:
Moving, Household—Fiction. | Best friends—Fiction. | Friendship—Fiction. |
Difference (Psychology)—Fiction.
Classification: LCC PZ7.J153555 Br 2016 | DDC 813.6—dc23
LC record available at http://lccn.loc.gov/2015049076

Design by Lori Bye

Printed and bound in Canada.
10009S17

Table of contents

Ash

Ashley "Ash" Sanchez may be small, but she's mighty! Ash likes to play all types of games — from sports to video games — and she loves to win. Ash may be loud and silly, but more than anything, she is a great friend!

Lee

Ashlee Taylor, otherwise known as Lee, is tall and graceful. When Lee is not twirling around in her dance classes, she can be found drawing or painting. Lee may be shy around new people, but she is as sweet and as kind as could be!

chapter one

{ BUSY GIRLS }

Eight-year-olds Ashley Sanchez and Ashlee Taylor were best friends. Although some knew them as Ashley Small and Ashlee Tall, most people called them Ash and Lee.

Ash and Lee were different in many ways. Ash was small and liked sports. Lee was tall and liked to dance. One thing they both liked was playing at the park.

Lee and Ash had lived across the hall from each other in the same apartment building until a month ago. Then Lee and her family moved to a house nearby. Their favorite park was in between Ash's apartment building and Lee's new house.

"Let's play hot lava!" Ash said when they got to the park. She raced to the top of the slide.

"Okay!" Lee said. She ran up behind Ash and looked around. "The ground is lava, so we can't touch it. Let's see if we can make it all the way to that bench." She pointed to the far edge of the park.

"Got it! Let's go," Ash said.

Ash was small, but she was strong.
When she reached the bottom of the
slide, she jumped across to the monkey
bars. Her feet never touched the ground
as she climbed along the jungle gym.

Lee was graceful. She had long legs. At the bottom of the slide, she leaped toward the merry-go-round. When she landed, it turned just enough for her to reach the swing. Lee was able to stretch her long arms and legs and climb onto the swing.

From the jungle gym and the swing, Ash and Lee needed to jump the same distance to reach the bench.

Lee asked, "Hey, Ash! Are you ready to jump?"

"Let's count to three," Ash said. "One, two, three!"

The girls jumped as far as they could. They both landed in the grass in front of the bench.

Ash did not like to lose. At first she was mad that she had not made it to the bench. Then she saw Lee rolling around in the grass and acting silly.

"Ahhh! The lava is so hot!" Lee yelled. She waved her arms in the air.

Ash laughed. She threw her arms into the air. "I'm melting!" she called.

The girls laughed and giggled.

"Let's try to reach something closer," Ash said.

Lee agreed, and they went back to the slide to start over again.

After a while, their moms called them over. Mrs. Sanchez and Mrs. Taylor were best friends, just like Ash and Lee. They liked to visit with each other at the park while the girls played.

"It's time to head home, Lee," Mrs. Taylor said.

"Maybe we can play on Wednesday?" Ash asked hopefully.

Lee shook her head. "I've got dance. How about Friday?"

"I have a basketball game," Ash said.

Ash and Lee frowned. Why was it so hard to find a time to get together?

"I'm sure we can figure something out," Mrs. Sanchez told the girls.

They said good-bye and headed in different directions. As they walked away, Ash and Lee looked back at each other and waved. Neither of them liked that they didn't know when they would see each other again.

chapter two

{ A GREAT IDEA }

A week and a half later, Lee's family went to Ash's house for dinner. As Mr. Sanchez opened the door, Ash raced past him. She wrapped her arms around Lee, who stood in the doorway with her family. Lee giggled and hugged her back.

"You two act as if you haven't seen each other in years!" Mr. Sanchez laughed.

"It feels like it," Ash said. "We used to see each other every day after school. It's bad enough that we're not in the same class. Now we don't ride the same bus!"

Lee nodded and followed Ash to the dining room table.

Mrs. Sanchez was a very good cook. She liked to make spicy food. Ash loved spicy food. Lee did not. Mrs. Sanchez always made a special plate for Lee that was just the way she liked it.

Ash ate quickly. She wanted to go play. Lee took her time.

When Lee finally finished, Mrs. Sanchez said, "Lee, I made your favorite chocolate chip cookies."

Lee smiled. She loved anything with chocolate. Ash didn't really like sweets, so she didn't have any cookies. While Lee enjoyed her dessert, Ash grew bored.

To pass the time, Ash made funny faces at her baby brother, Sam. He laughed and clapped his hands. As Ash made sillier and sillier faces, Sam laughed more and more. He got so excited, he grabbed a handful of crumbs off of his tray. He threw them into the air. The crumbs landed on Lee's older sister, Mallory.

"Hey!" Mallory cried, picking crumbs out of her hair.

Ash and Lee tried not to laugh, but they couldn't help it. Mallory looked so funny with crumbs all over her.

Mrs. Sanchez jumped up to help clean off Mallory. "Why don't you two go play?" she said to Ash and Lee.

Ash and Lee hopped up. They hurried down the hall to Ash's room.

"Did you see Mallory's face?" Lee asked. "She spent an hour doing her hair before we came over!"

Ash began to feel bad. "I hope she's not mad."

Lee shook her head. "My parents said she could go to the movies with her friends after dinner. She will forget all about it."

Lee looked around Ash's room. Something seemed different since the last time she had been there.

"Is that a new blanket?" Lee asked.

"Yep," Ash said. "And new curtains."

Lee frowned. "I guess it's been a long time since I've been here."

Ash frowned too. "It has. I wish you still lived across the hall. I miss you."

"I miss you too," Lee told her. "I wish we could spend more time together."

"Me too. But we are both so busy," Ash said.

Suddenly Lee had an idea. "Hey! What if we did an activity together? Then we could see each other all the time."

"Great idea," Ash said, a big smile on her face. "I bet finding something we both like to do will be easy!"

chapter three

{ BASKETBALL BLUES }

A few mornings later, Ash and Lee had plans to meet at the neighborhood park again.

Lee and her mom were running late. Ash sat on the bench next to her mom and Sam. She was so excited. She couldn't sit still.

"You are full of energy today!" her mom said.

When Ash spotted Lee and her mom across the park, she couldn't wait. She jumped up and ran to meet them.

Lee noticed that Ash was carrying a basketball.

"I know what we can do!" Ash said as soon as she got to Lee.

"Well, hello to you too!" Lee teased her friend.

"I'm too excited to say hi," Ash said. "I thought of an activity we can do together!"

Now Lee was excited too. "What is it?" she asked.

Ash held up the basketball. "You can join my basketball team," she said, smiling. "We are always looking for good players. I can teach you how to play! Then we would have practice together twice a week."

Lee wasn't too sure about Ash's idea. She had tried playing a few sports before. They weren't her thing. But she did want to spend more time with her best friend.

"Okay," she said. "I'll give it a try."

The pair headed over to the basketball courts.

"The first thing you need to learn is how to dribble the basketball," Ash explained as they walked.

When they got to the court, Ash bounced the ball. She was very good. She even dribbled the ball between her legs.

Lee said, "It looks like fun!"

Ash passed Lee the ball. Lee tried to dribble, but the ball bounced off her foot and rolled away. She giggled and chased after it. She tried again, using both hands to bounce the ball high into the air.

"No, no, no," Ash told her. She took the ball from Lee and began dribbling. "That's against the rules. You can only use one hand. And you keep the ball low to the ground so no one can steal it."

Lee hopped over and took the ball from Ash. "Like this?" she asked. Then Lee ran away with the ball. "Let's play keep away!"

"No!" Ash yelled, running after Lee. "That's not how you play basketball!"

Lee held the ball high above her head. She twirled around and around. "Try to steal it from me!" she shouted.

Ash frowned. She was frustrated that Lee wasn't playing by the rules. "Let me show you how to shoot the ball," she said.

Lee handed her the ball.

"Hold it like this, with your elbows in," Ash said. "Then push your arm up and flap your wrist, like you're waving bye."

Ash shot the ball. It made a *swish* as it went through the net.

"Got it," Lee said. But she didn't shoot the ball the way Ash had. Instead, she spread her feet wide and held the ball with both hands. Then she lowered the ball between her legs and flung it toward the basket. The ball flew up and over the basket and landed in the field behind it.

As Lee chased the ball, she called, "You're right! Basketball is fun!"

Ash shook her head. She mumbled, "Maybe basketball won't be our activity after all."

chapter four

{ COOKIES & CANVAS }

As Lee and Ash walked back to find their moms, they tried to think of another activity they could do together.

"I'm sorry basketball didn't work," Lee said.

Ash had been frustrated, but she wasn't mad at Lee. "It's okay," she said.

As they walked, the girls came upon a large bulletin board filled with fliers.

One of the fliers caught Lee's attention. She pointed to it and said, "Hey, look at this one! It's for something called Cookies and Canvas."

Ash was confused. "Cookies and canvas? What is that all about?"

Lee read the flier and grew more excited. "A local art studio is going to have a painting class for kids," she said. "Each person gets her own canvas and takes home her own painting."

Lee loved art! She looked hopefully at Ash and said, "Maybe painting could be our activity?"

Ash didn't like cookies or art very much. But since they hadn't come up with any other ideas, she said, "Sure, why not?"

* * *

It was the afternoon of the painting class and Lee was excited. She didn't like to get messy, so she wore her art smock over her clothes. She asked her mom if they could go early so she could find a spot near the front. Ash arrived just as the class was starting. She didn't have a seat at first, which made her grumpy. When she finally found one, she slumped onto it and almost knocked her canvas over.

Their teacher was named Janet. "We
are going to have so much fun today,"
Janet told the class. She explained that
she'd paint along on her canvas. She'd
share what colors and brushes to use.

"Your painting doesn't have to look exactly like mine," Janet said. "My picture is an example. Feel free to paint your canvas however you'd like."

As Janet spoke, Lee organized her art supplies. She liked to keep her work area neat. She noticed that Ash's brushes were pointing in different directions. "You may want to face them all the same way," Lee whispered. "It makes them easier to grab while you're working."

Ash nodded but didn't fix her brushes. She was listening closely to Janet. She wanted to make sure she painted her picture just right.

Finally, it was time for them to start painting. They were going to paint a field of flowers. Lee followed along but chose different colors and shapes for her flowers. She was having a great time.

Ash was not having a great time. Her painting didn't look anything like Janet's, and that bothered her. The more she tried to fix it, the worse it got.

Lee saw Ash frowning. "What's wrong?" she asked.

"My painting is awful," Ash said.

"No, it's not," Lee told her. "It looks really good!"

Ash reached across her work area for a bigger brush. She knocked over the cup of water she was using to clean her brushes. Water spilled over onto Lee's work area. It made a mess.

"Oh!" Lee cried. She began to clean up the mess.

"I'm sorry!" Ash said.

"It's okay," Lee said. She wished that Ash had fixed her brushes like she had suggested.

Ash was frustrated. She wanted her painting to look like Janet's, and it looked completely different.

After they had finished cleaning up the mess, Ash dipped a big brush into the yellow paint.

As she raised the brush, Lee said, "That's too much paint!" But it was too late. As Ash slapped the brush on the canvas, paint splattered everywhere. Drops of it landed on Lee's painting and on both of their faces.

Ash felt awful. She didn't want Lee to be mad at her. She looked over at Lee to apologize. When they saw how funny they each looked with paint on their faces, they burst out laughing.

chapter five

{ SNACKS WITH THE DADS }

Lee loved to run errands with her dad. When they finished what they needed to do, they always stopped at their favorite coffee shop for a treat.

A few days after the messy painting class, Lee and her dad were finishing their list of things to do. As they got out of the car, Lee heard someone calling her name.

"Lee!" It was Ash. She and her dad were just leaving the hardware store next to the coffee shop.

"Ash!" Lee cheered. "We're going to get a treat at the coffee shop. Want to join us?"

Ash looked at her dad. "Can we?"

"Sounds good," Mr. Sanchez said with a smile. "I could use some coffee."

The girls were so happy to see each other. They found a table while their dads ordered. Lee always got a hot chocolate and a chocolate chip muffin. Ash got cranberry juice and a blueberry muffin.

As they enjoyed their yummy snacks, the girls told their dads about how hard it was to find an activity to do together.

"Lee ended up creating a new game called Keep-Away Basketball." Ash laughed. "I don't think she'd be allowed to play that way on my team!"

"Painting didn't work, either," Lee told them. "When we left, we looked like we had giant yellow freckles!"

Ash and Lee laughed. Hot chocolate almost came out of Lee's nose!

After they had realized that painting wasn't going to be their activity, they had fun at the class. They signed each other's paintings and agreed to hang them in their bedrooms.

"It sure would be nice for you girls to find something to do together," Mr. Taylor said.

"I've got an idea," Mr. Sanchez said. "When I was at the community center, I saw a sign for a gymnastics class. That might be fun."

Ash and Lee both shook their heads.

"We tried a sport," Lee said. "It didn't work out so well."

"Gymnastics is so much more than a sport," Mr. Taylor said. "Lee, I think you'd really like the tumbling and the balance beam. It's a lot like dancing."

"I'm not a good dancer," Ash said, shaking her head. "Lee said I've got two left feet!"

Mr. Sanchez chuckled. "But you are a good athlete. I could see you enjoying the uneven bars and the vault. They both require a lot of strength and attention."

The girls looked at each other. They were not so sure about gymnastics.

"Why don't you give it a try?" Mr. Sanchez suggested. "You can take one class. If you don't like it, we won't sign you up for any more."

Ash leaned over and whispered to Lee, "What do you think?"

Lee shrugged. "I'll do it if you do it."

Ash sat back and said to their dads, "We'll do it!"

chapter six

{ TOGETHER TIME }

Ash and Lee were nervous on the day of their first gymnastics class. As they walked into the gym, they saw the different equipment and colorful mats. There were lots of other kids in the class. Some were doing flips and cartwheels on the mats. They already looked like gymnasts.

The instructors called everyone over to the mat for stretching. They formed a big circle. Ash and Lee stood next to each other.

After they had stretched, one of the instructors explained that the class would be split into two groups. She said that they would be working at two stations that day, tumbling and uneven bars. Ash and Lee locked arms. They did not want to be separated. Thankfully, they ended up in the same group.

Their group headed over to the tumbling mat. The instructor explained that they would be doing cartwheels.

She showed them how to plant their hands on the ground while kicking their feet up into the air. When she was done, she said they would each try a cartwheel.

"We can do that," Ash said to Lee. She went to get in line. When she noticed Lee wasn't coming with her, she stopped. "What's wrong?"

Lee didn't move. "I don't want to do it," she said.

"Why not?" Ash asked. "You can do a cartwheel."

Lee looked scared. "I don't want to do it in front of everyone."

"You dance in front of people all the time. I've seen you do it," Ash said.

"Yes, but that's after lots of practice. I've never done cartwheels like that before," Lee said.

Ash thought for a moment. Then she said, "I'll go first. Watch, it will be fine."

Ash and Lee got in line. When it was Ash's turn, she did three cartwheels. On the first, she rotated too much and fell down. On the second, she tipped over halfway through. Ash was determined to get it right. By the last one, she did a perfect cartwheel.

Ash's cartwheels had looked sort of funny. Lee was happy to see that no one had laughed.

Ash stood at the other end of the mat. She gave Lee a big thumbs-up and a smile. Lee took a deep breath. Then she did three perfect cartwheels, with very little help from the instructor.

"You did it!" Ash said.

"That was fun!" Lee exclaimed. They high-fived and got back in line. They ended up having a great time tumbling.

When they switched to the bars, it was Ash's turn to be nervous.

"They are so high," she said to Lee.

"Not really," Lee told her.

"Maybe not for you!" Ash replied.

"You can do this. I've seen you swing from the top of the jungle gym a million times!" Lee said.

"Okay," Ash said, but she was still nervous.

Ash walked over to the bars. The instructor helped her up to the top bar. At first she was worried about falling. She looked down and saw Lee smiling and waving. Ash relaxed a little. The instructor showed her how to use her legs to swing back and forth. Once she got going, she had so much fun! The bars were definitely going to be her favorite.

After class, Ash and Lee met their dads outside of the gym.

"Well?" asked Mr. Taylor.

Ash and Lee looked at each other. "I thought it was fun!" said Lee.

"Yeah, we even got to do cartwheels!" Ash said.

Lee nodded. She said, "But I think the best part about it is that we got to hang out together."

Ash hugged her friend and said, "I agree!"

GLOSSARY

activity (ak-TIV-i-tee) — something that you do

apologize (uh-PAH-luh-jize) — to say you're sorry

canvas (KAN-vuhs) — a strong piece of cloth stretched over a wooden frame for painting

cartwheels (KAHRT-weels) — circular, sideways handsprings with arms and legs extended

dribble (DRIB-uhl) — in basketball, to bounce the ball while walking or running

energy (EN-ur-jee) — the strength to do things without getting tired

equipment (ee-KWIP-muhnt) — the tools, machines, or products needed for a certain purpose

errands (ER-uhnds) — short journeys that involve delivering or collecting something

frustrated (FRUHS-tray-tid) — feeling helpless or discouraged

gymnastics (jim-NAS-tiks) — physical exercise, often performed on special equipment such as ropes, mats, or bars

instructor (in-STRUHK-tor) — a person who teaches something

lava (LAH-vuh) — the hot, liquid rock that pours out of a volcano when it erupts

supplies (SUH-plize) — things that are needed for a particular purpose or activity

TALK IT OUT

1. Ash and Lee are best friends, but they enjoy different activities. Do you think gymnastics is a good activity for Ash and Lee to do together? Discuss why or why not using examples from the text.

2. When Ash tries to get Lee to play basketball, Lee acts silly. Talk about why you think she acted that way. How would you have felt if you were Lee in that situation? What about if you were Ash?

3. Imagine that when the book ends, Ash and Lee still haven't found an activity they can do together. What advice would you give them for finding something they both enjoy?

WRITE IT DOWN

1. Both Ash and Lee felt nervous to try new hobbies in this book. Have you ever felt nervous to try a new activity? Write a paragraph about what activity you were trying. Explain why you felt nervous at first and how you felt after.

2. What do you like to do for fun? Write a list of your favorite activities, explaining why you enjoy each of them.

3. Ash feels frustrated when she can't make her painting look like the instructor's. Have you ever felt frustrated while trying a new activity? Write a paragraph about your experience.

HOW WELL DO YOU KNOW YOUR BEST FRIEND?

Ashley and Ashlee may be different from one another, but they know each other very well! Even when we know our friends well, we can be surprised to learn new things about them. Take this quiz with your best friend to see if there's anything you don't yet know about him or her.

what you need

- Pen or pencil
- Paper

what you do

Take the quiz about your best friend's likes and dislikes. Write down your answers, keeping them hidden from your BFF. When you're done, you can share them and see if you learn anything new about one another!

1. Where was your BFF born?

2. What is his/her favorite food?

3. What is his/her least favorite food?

4. How many siblings does your BFF have?

5. What's his/her favorite book?

6. If your BFF could travel anywhere, where would he/she go?

7. When is your BFF's birthday?

8. Who does your BFF look up to most?

9. What is your best friend's favorite color?

10. Name his/her favorite band or singer.

11. If your BFF could have one superpower, what would it be?

12. What is your BFF's greatest fear?

13. Can your BFF speak another language? If so, what is it?

14. What would your best friend's perfect day be like?

15. If your BFF was going to be stuck on a desert island, what three things would he or she most want to take along?

ABOUT THE AUTHOR

Michele Jakubowski has the teachers in her life to thank for her love of reading and writing. While writing has always been a passion for Michele, she believes it is the books she has read throughout the years, and the teachers who assigned them, that have made her the storyteller she is today. Raised in the Chicago suburb of Hoffman Estates, Michele now lives in Powell, Ohio, with her husband, John, and their children, Jack and Mia.

ABOUT THE ILLUSTRATOR

Born in Transylvania, Hédi Fekete grew up watching and drawing her favorite cartoon characters. Each night, her mother read her beautiful bedtime stories, which made her love for storytelling grow. Hédi's love for books and animation stuck with her through the years, inspiring her to become an illustrator, digital artist, and animator.

THE FUN DOESN'T STOP HERE!

Discover more at *www.capstonekids.com*

Videos and Contests
Games and Puzzles
Friends and Favorites
Authors and Illustrators

Find cool websites and more books like this one
at *www.facthound.com*. Just type in the
Book ID: 9781515800101 and you're ready to go!